Disney · PIXAR

Disney·PIXAR

Hachette

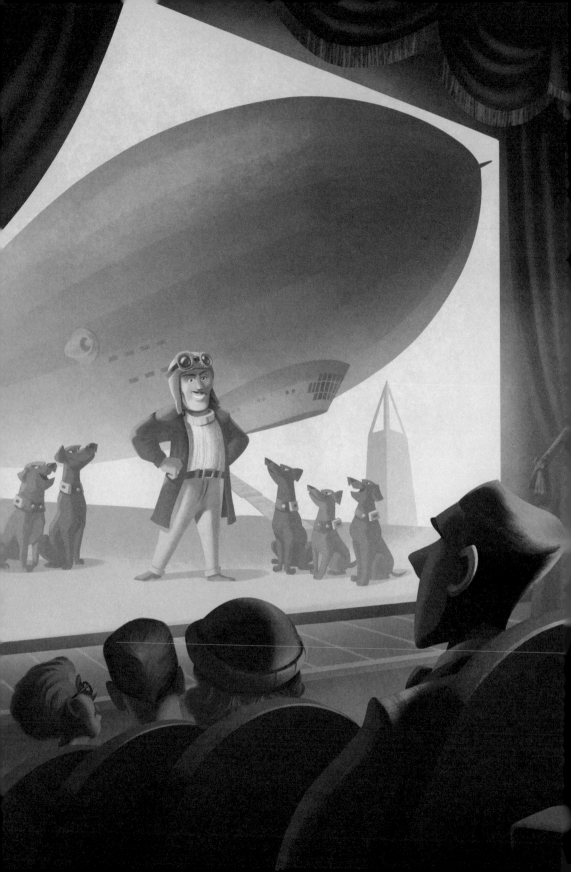

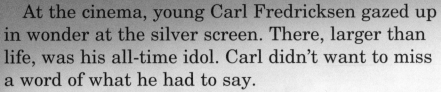

At the cinema, young Carl Fredricksen gazed up in wonder at the silver screen. There, larger than life, was his all-time idol. Carl didn't want to miss a word of what he had to say.

Charles Muntz, the famous explorer, was about to board his airship and set off for South America in search of a mysterious creature known as 'The Monster of Paradise Falls'.

"Adventure is out there!" declared Muntz. Carl dreamed that one day he would be an explorer, just like his hero.

As Carl walked home, still dreaming of being an explorer, he heard a shout: "Adventure is out there!" The voice came from a derelict house. Carl decided to investigate.

In the house, a girl called Ellie was piloting her
own imaginary airship. When she saw Carl in his
helmet and goggles, she realised that he was an
explorer, just like her! She pinned a badge, made
from a grape-soda bottle cap, onto his shirt.
"You and me. We're in a club now," she explained.

Straightaway, Carl and Ellie had their first
adventure – but he fell and broke his arm! To cheer
him up, Ellie showed him her adventure book.

"Charles Muntz...explorer," said Ellie. "When I
get big, I'm going where he's going: South America."
Ellie had even drawn a picture of the house, parked
right next to the Paradise Falls.

Carl promised that he would take her to her
dream location one day.

From that day, Carl and Ellie were best friends. And when they grew up, they got married and moved into the house where they had first met.

The years went by and Carl and Ellie grew old.
They never did get round to becoming explorers.
When Ellie died, Carl was alone in the big
house. Nothing was the same without his beloved
Ellie. Even the neighbourhood was changing. All
the old houses were being pulled down to make
way for bigger, modern buildings.

One day, a boy in uniform knocked at Carl's door. "My name is Russell, and I am a Junior Wilderness Explorer. Are you in need of assistance today, sir?" he asked.

Russell was keen to earn his Assisting the Elderly badge, but Carl just wanted this pest to leave him in peace. He sent Russell off on a mission to track down a bird called a snipe, that had been eating his flowers. But there was no such bird – Carl had made the story up to get rid of Russell.

Alone again at last, Carl leafed through Ellie's adventure book. He felt even more miserable than usual, because he was going to be forced out of his house and sent to live in a retirement home.

Carl decided that the time had come to take action. He had a wonderful idea...

The next day, when
two nurses from
the home came to
collect Carl, they
couldn't believe
their eyes. Carl's
house, attached
to hundreds
and hundreds
of balloons, was
floating high up
into the air!

"We're on our
way, Ellie!" cried
Carl happily, as he
plotted his course for
South America.

KNOCK! KNOCK! KNOCK!

Carl was startled. Who could be knocking at the door? The house was flying thousands of feet up in the air! It was Russell, who had been searching for the snipe under Carl's house when it took off.

Carl decided he would have to land to let Russell off. But just then, a massive storm broke.

Carl tried to avoid the storm, but it was too late.

As the house was tossed around, Carl tried desperately to save Ellie's things. Eventually he gave up, and fell asleep, exhausted.

At last, Carl woke up.

"I steered the house!" said Russell proudly.
"We're in South America!"

Just then, the house landed with a bump, and
they both tumbled off the porch. Then the house
began to rise up again, and Carl had to grab the
garden hose to stop his home from floating away.

Carl looked around. To his amazement, he
realised he was looking at Paradise Falls – and it
looked just as it did in Ellie's book!

"We made it!" yelled Carl happily.

The house was too high off the ground for them to clamber back on, so the pair decided to walk to the falls, pulling the house along, using the garden hose. On the way, Russell met a giant, multicoloured bird, who he decided to call Kevin. The bird seemed to be friendly and, like Russell, it loved chocolate!

Russell wanted to keep the bird, but Carl refused. As they set off again for the Falls, Russell secretly dropped a trail of chocolate, so that the bird would follow them.

A little further on, Carl and Russell came across a dog.

"Hi there," said the dog. "My name is Dug." Dug explained that his master made him a hi-tech collar that allowed him to talk. Dug also said he was on a special mission to find a bird.

At that moment, Kevin appeared.

"That's the bird!" exclaimed Dug. "May I take your bird back to camp as my prisoner?"

But Russell didn't want to lose his new friend. He made Carl promise not to let the bird be taken.

Eventually, they all set off again, with Dug still trying to persuade Kevin to be his prisoner!

The next morning, Kevin was calling out sadly. Dug explained that she needed to go home to her chicks. Russell was amazed. Kevin was a girl! The group carried on their journey without her.

As they made their way towards the Falls, three
fierce dogs leapt out from some bushes.
"Where's the bird?" snarled one of the dogs.
When they found out that Dug had let the bird
escape, the dogs demanded that the threesome
return with them to their master. The
dogs bared their teeth menacingly.
The group realised they had no
choice but to obey...

The dogs led the group to a cave. At the entrance stood an old man, surrounded by dogs. When he saw the man, Carl exclaimed: "Wait...are you Charles Muntz?" Carl couldn't believe he was meeting his childhood hero!

Muntz was pleased to have guests, so he invited them into his home. He showed them the skeleton of a giant bird.

"I've spent a lifetime tracking it," he explained.

"Hey, that looks like Kevin!" cried Russell.

"You know this bird?" said Muntz suspiciously. Carl realised that he and Russell were in danger. Muntz, furious because he thought that Carl and Russell wanted to steal the bird from him, let the pack of dogs loose.

Luckily, Kevin arrived just in time to save Carl and Russell.

The pair leapt onto Kevin's back and, with Dug's help, they managed to get out of the cave. But outside, they found themselves at the edge of a cliff, with the pack of dogs hot on their heels. They were trapped!

Luckily, a gust of wind lifted the house, with the friends clinging onto the hose below it, into the air and away from the dogs. They were safe!

But the friends hadn't reckoned on the
cunning of Charles Muntz. He had tracked them
down in the *Spirit of Adventure*. Muntz threw his
lantern at the house, starting a fire.

Carl had to choose between saving Kevin or his
house. He rushed to put out the flames and Kevin
was captured and bundled into the airship.

Inside the house, Carl found Ellie's adventure book. To his surprise, the pages at the back of the book weren't blank. They were full of pictures of their life together.

Ellie had written a message below the last photo: *Thanks for the adventure. Now go have a new one. Love, Ellie.*

Suddenly, Carl heard a noise on the roof. He hurried outside, just in time to see Russell rising into the air, holding a large bunch of balloons.

"I'm gonna help Kevin even if you won't!" Russell called to Carl.

"No, Russell!" Carl cried, and tried to set off after him. But the house wouldn't budge. Frustrated, Carl tossed a chair off the porch. The house rose a little. This gave Carl an idea.

He began throwing everything out of the house until it was light enough to take off into the air.

Carl set off after Russell, who had been captured by Muntz and imprisoned on the airship.

Using the garden hose like a rope, Carl swung the house over to the airship and managed to rescue Russell.

With Russell safe inside the house, Carl set off to free Kevin. But first he had to deal with the fierce dogs who were guarding Kevin's cage.

Carl took a ball from his walking cane and shouted: "Who wants the ball?" He threw the ball and the dogs chased off after it. With the dogs out of the way, he could finally free Kevin.

Suddenly, Muntz appeared, waving a huge sword. The two men began to fight.

Meanwhile, Russell was trying to defend the house from dogs in fighter planes!

Carl finally managed to free Kevin, and they joined Russell and Dug in the house. But then some balloons burst and the house crashed onto the roof of the airship. Carl fell out of the house, while Muntz ran in to get Kevin. The house was teetering dangerously on the edge of the ship.

"Everyone hang on to Kevin!" Carl yelled. He waved some chocolate at Kevin. The bird ran towards it and leapt through the window, taking Russell and Dug with her. Muntz tried to grab Kevin, but his foot got caught on a bunch of balloons and he drifted away.

Carl and Russell took Kevin back to her family. After a brief stop to meet the chicks, the two adventurers, accompanied by Dug, set off for home aboard the *Spirit of Adventure*.

Carl may have lost his house, but he had gained two new friends.

At last, the adventure was over. Russell had truly earned his Assisting the Elderly badge.

On the day of the ceremony, Carl came up to the stage to pin on Russell's badge. He had an extra surprise for Russell – the grape-soda cap badge that Ellie had given him all those years ago!

"Russell, for assisting the elderly, and for performing above and beyond the call of duty, I would like to award you the highest honour I can bestow: the Ellie Badge," said Carl.

Russell smiled proudly, knowing that the friends had many more adventures together in store.